The Case of the
WANDERING
WEREWOLF

Drew Stevenson

Illustrated by Linda Winchester

A MINSTREL® BOOK

PUBLISHED BY POCKET BOOKS

New York   London   Toronto   Sydney   Tokyo   Singapore

For Mark,
my brother and my friend

 A Minstrel Book published by
POCKET BOOKS, a division of Simon & Schuster
1230 Avenue of the Americas, New York, NY 10020

ISBN: 0-671-67238-X

First Minstrel Books printing February 1991

10 9 8 7 6 5 4 3 2 1

A MINSTREL BOOK and colophon are registered trademarks
of Simon & Schuster

Printed in U.S.A.

"It's not easy being a believer, Raymond.
I know. I've been one all my life."

—J. Huntley English, M.H.

1

"Raymond! Raymond Almond!"

I stopped in the middle of the crowded sidewalk and looked back to see who was calling my name. At first all I saw was a mob of kids trying to get around me. It was a bitterly cold January day, and the wind outside the Barkley Central School District buildings was enough to make a polar bear put on long underwear. Classes were over for the week, and no one was wasting any time hurrying home if they walked to school, or getting on the school buses if they lived in the country.

"Raymond! Hey, Raymond!"

I began to think someone was playing a joke on me. All I could see were hats and scarves and gloves and heavy coats and the steam from a hundred chattering mouths coming at me.

"Ouch!" I cried as someone's boot crunched down on my foot.

Even before I looked, I knew who the tootsie masher was. Who else? Verna Wilkes! In the Garden of Eden, Verna Wilkes would be a weed. She's a gutter ball in the bowling game of life. And on top of that, she's stuck up. As I looked into her snooty face, I could tell she had stepped on my foot on purpose.

"Watch it, Verna!" I growled.

"You know something, Raymond?" Verna said, tapping her forehead with her mitten. "The longer I know you, the more I think you're a few cans of soda short of a full six pack."

With that, she moved away in the crowd. As usual, I couldn't think of anything snappy to say back at her so I started limping along with the rest of the kids. I figured she had called my name so I would stop and she could step on my foot. I was surprised to hear the same voice *behind* me again.

"Raymond! Wait up!"

I stopped and looked back. This time I saw a kid waving his hand at me. I didn't know his name but I knew he was in the fourth grade. Since I'm in the seventh grade, I don't know many fourth graders. I'm tall for my age but, as I watched him fight his way toward me, I could see he was short for his.

"Hi!" he said, offering me his hand. "My name is Tony Chipaletta. My friends call me Chips."

"Hello," I muttered, as I shook his hand. I was

kind of miffed that this fourth grader had given Verna the Toe Masher a chance to do her stuff.

"I need to talk to you in private," he went on.

I really wanted to give this kid the brush off, but that isn't my style. It wasn't too long ago that *I* was in the fourth grade. Besides, I was curious.

"Follow me," I said, leading him out of the kid traffic onto the lawn. We plowed through the snow until we reached a huge tree at the corner of the junior-high building.

"All right," I said leaning against the thick trunk. "What can I do for you?"

The boy stared at his boots and shivered.

"Look!" I said impatiently, shivering with him. "I'm cold, too! Talk to me so we can both go get warm."

The boy looked up at me.

"I'm . . . I'm not cold." He shivered again. "I'm scared."

Now I noticed the tears in his eyes. I put my hands on his shoulders to steady him.

"Scared of what?"

The boy took a deep breath.

"Something tried to kill me last night in Lost Woods."

I shivered again, and this time it wasn't because of the cold.

9

2

"What?" I cried in amazement. "Someone tried to kill you last night?"

The boy sniffed and shook his head.

"No, I said some*thing* tried to kill me."

"Some*thing?*" I gulped.

Chips looked over his shoulder at the line of buses.

"I gotta go," he said. "My bus is gonna leave. Come to my house tonight and I'll tell you more. Please!"

"Hey, wait a second!" I called out to him as he ran toward the buses. "Where do you live?"

"Locust Grove Trailer Park," he called back. "Lot Twelve."

As I watched him climb onto his bus, I wondered what this kid was talking about. And why was he telling me? It sounded like a matter for Police Chief Murphy, not Raymond Almond, the Sometimes Nervous.

Suddenly two huge hands clamped down on my shoulders and spun me around. I found myself looking up at Bucky Bovine. I groaned. What a day! First Verna Wilkes squashes my foot. Then some kid tells me that something tried to kill him last night in Lost Woods. And now I'm grabbed by a kid who looks like a cross between King Kong and Hulk Hogan.

Bucky Bovine is in the eighth grade and plays defensive tackle on our school's football team. He looks like a lineman, too! Big and strong. And now, for some reason, he had hold of me like I was some poor quarterback.

"I wanna talk to you, Walnut," Bucky growled, pulling my face close to his. "What was that twerp talking to you about?"

"Hi, Bucky." I tried to smile. "What's up?"

"You heard me, Acorn," he hissed. "What were you doing, hanging around here with Chipaletta?"

No one has ever accused me of being too brave. Especially when I'm facing someone who reminds me of a bulldozer. But that Chipaletta kid had looked real scared and I wasn't about to squeal on him.

"He . . . he wanted me to help him with his homework," I lied.

"Your name may be Almond but I'm going to turn you into *peanut* butter," Bucky threatened.

I closed my eyes, gritted my teeth, and wondered if he could really mash me into sandwich spread.

11

"Ahhhhh!" Bucky suddenly yelled as he let me go.

I opened my eyes and saw him hopping around like a huge toad.

I can't think of too many times in my life when I've been glad to see Verna Wilkes. This was definitely one of them. I didn't know where she had come from, but she had stomped on Bucky's foot just in time to save my life.

"What's the matter with you, Wilkes?" Bucky bellowed.

"You know something, Bovine?" Verna said, tapping her forehead with her mitten. "I don't think your elevator goes all the way to the top floor."

"Why, you . . ." Bucky raised his fists and stepped forward.

Verna stuck out her jaw and dug in. I was bracing myself for World War III when the sound of motors gave me an idea.

"Hey, Bucky," I yelled, pointing. "Your bus is leaving."

"Hey, wait up!" he cried, running across the lawn.

He stopped at the curb and looked back.

"You, Almond, stay away from Chipaletta! And you, Wilkes, I'll settle with you later!"

"Thanks for saving my life, Verna," I said as we watched the buses pulling out.

"Don't flatter yourself, Raymond," she answered in that snooty voice of hers. "I just don't like to see an eighth grader picking on a seventh grader. Even if the seventh grader happens to be you."

With that she walked off toward her house. Since I live near her, I let her get a lead and then followed.

"What else bad can happen?" I wondered gloomily.

If I had known then about the mystery that was about to involve me, I never would have asked that question.

13

After school, I delivered the *Observer-Reporter* to my customers. As I trudged along through the cold with my bag of newspapers, I kept thinking about Chips Chipaletta. He had said some*thing,* not some*one,* had tried to kill him last night in Lost Woods.

What did he mean by something? Who, or what, would want to hurt a kid like that? And why didn't Bucky Bovine want me talking to Chips? Was he mixed up in this somehow?

By the time I delivered my last paper, it was dark and I was thinking about Lost Woods, this big forest outside of town. Even on a sunny summer's day, Lost Woods is plenty gloomy. I couldn't imagine how spooky it must be on a dark winter's night. Sure I was curious about Chips Chipaletta and his strange story. But I wasn't sure if I was curious enough to walk out to the Locust Grove Trailer Park—which, by the way, sits on the edge of those woods. And on a freezing night like this! Especially when I knew that Bucky Bovine also lived out that way somewhere.

Dad had made a big pot of chili for supper. I was grateful for our warm cozy kitchen as Dad, Mom, and I sat at the table, dipping fresh Italian bread from Krency's Bakery into our steaming bowls. My little brother sat in a highchair next to me. I didn't even mind that he kept fishing kidney beans out of his chili and throwing them at me.

For dessert, we had ice cream from Majersky's Ice Cream Parlor. My little brother quickly ate his scoop and then began sniffling when Mom wouldn't give him another. I looked at the tears in his eyes and remembered the tears that Chips Chipaletta had fought to hold back. That fourth grader was scared, and he had come to me for help.

As I left the kitchen, I decided to call him. Why couldn't he talk to me over the phone and save me the trip out there? I found the number in the phone book and dialed. The line was busy. I waited and tried again. Still busy.

I thought about Chips sitting at home waiting for me to come. That did it.

"Mom," I called out. "I'm going over to Tony Chipaletta's house for awhile."

I made it sound like Chips lived nearby.

"Don't be late," Mom warned. "And bundle up."

15

I did just that and stepped out the front door. It was bitter cold, but at least there was no wind. Also, it wasn't as dark as I thought it would be. A quarter moon was floating above the houses, adding to the light from the street lamps.

I walked fast to keep warm. Barkley, Pennsylvania, is a small town. Walk in any direction and you're soon in the country. As I hiked out the Washington Pike, the street lights stopped and I was glad for the light of the moon. Houses gave way to farms. I looked at the lighted windows and wished I was inside the warmth.

I had never been to the Locust Grove Trailer Park but I knew where it was. About a mile out the Pike, I turned left onto a narrow road that cut through the woods. The trees grew right to the road's edge and blocked out the moon. I wished a car would come by to brighten my path and break the dead quiet.

After a quarter of a mile, the road widened and sloped downward. I stopped to get my bearings. At the bottom of the hill, the trailer park was spread out along short neat streets. But I wasn't looking at the trailers then. I was looking at what stretched beyond them for miles. Lost Woods!

As I gazed at those dark, thick, spooky miles of trees, it was easy to believe that something *could* be hiding in them. Something waiting to attack. Something deadly!

I tore my eyes away from the woods and walked down the road into the park. All the trailers were large and well cared for. I found the one on Lot 12, stepped up on the porch, and knocked at the door. It was quickly opened by a short, thin woman who spoke very good English with an Italian accent.

"Come in, come in," she invited. "You must be Raymond. Tony said you would be coming."

I smiled to myself as I took off my boots, while Mrs. Chipaletta hung up my coat. It seemed Tony had been more sure that I would come than I had been myself.

"Would you like something to eat?" Mrs. Chipaletta asked as she nodded toward the stove in the kitchen. "We always keep the sauce simmering. Mr. Chipaletta works the evening shift at the Jessop Steel Company, so we all eat at different times."

17

I told her no thank you as I stepped into the warm, comfortable living room. A small dog came up for a petting. A large furry cat on the couch looked at me and yawned.

"Tony's in his room down the hall on the left," Mrs. Chipaletta told me. "If you change your mind about some food, just holler."

I found Chips looking out the window in his bedroom. I felt as if I had stepped into a zoo. To the left, an aquarium filled with colorful tropical fish bubbled merrily. On the dresser, two hamsters played in a small cage. To the right, a pair of pretty parakeets chirped happily in their cage. And, to top it off, the dog and cat had followed me into the room.

Chip's face lit up when he saw me.

"Raymond! Thanks for coming!"

"So what's going on?" I asked. "I can't stay long."

Chips shook his head.

"I want to take you out in the woods and show you where it happened. I think it will make more sense."

My whole body stiffened like over-starched underwear.

"Out in the woods?" I squeaked. "*Lost* Woods?"

Chips nodded. "Come on."

I stepped over the cat and tripped over the dog as I followed him to the front door.

"Mom?" he called into the kitchen. "I'm going to show Raymond around outside. Okay?"

"Dress warmly and don't be gone long," Mrs. Chipaletta called back, sounding like my mom.

After bundling up, we stepped out into the cold, taking care to keep the cat and dog inside. Chips was silent as he led me to the end of his street. Past the last trailer, a small wooden footbridge crossed a creek. Beside the creek I could see a narrow path that disappeared into the woods.

I followed Chips across the bridge but froze as he started along the path. Every bone in my body was telling me to go home and drink hot chocolate where it was warm and safe.

When he realized I wasn't behind him, Chips stopped and looked back. He seemed so small, standing there. I knew that if this fourth grader wasn't afraid to go on, then I couldn't turn back either.

"It sure isn't easy being a seventh grader," I sighed to myself as I started after him.

5

The path turned into a rough trail as it wound along the creek, deeper and deeper into the woods. The trees were so thick above us that the moon's silvery rays did little to brighten the gloom. Chips switched on the flashlight he had brought.

As I followed him, I was glad that he seemed to know where he was going. The woods aren't called Lost for nothing! As long as I can remember, kids had been telling stories about people getting lost in these woods and never being seen again. I knew that, far to my left, Lost Woods ended at another cheery place called Lost Swamp. Last spring I had had some very scary moments in Lost Swamp. Now I didn't know which was worse. The swamp or the woods.

Chips and I had to move slowly because the snow and ice made the going slippery. As we walked along, I thought about what my dad had told me. He had lived in Barkley all his life, and he said that he'd never heard of anyone's really disappearing in either Lost Woods or Lost Swamp. But in those creepy woods that night, my father seemed very far away.

After awhile, we came to a place where another creek emptied into the first one. Chips suddenly stopped. I thought he was just catching his breath.

"I heard that there are abandoned mine shafts scattered all over these woods," I whispered.

"There are." Chips nodded. "You have to be careful where you walk. That's why I try to keep to the trails."

He pointed his flashlight along the second creek bank. I thought he was going to show me a mine shaft or something.

"Look there!" he cried, as he held the light steady.

I saw a large piece of metal lying half buried in the snow.

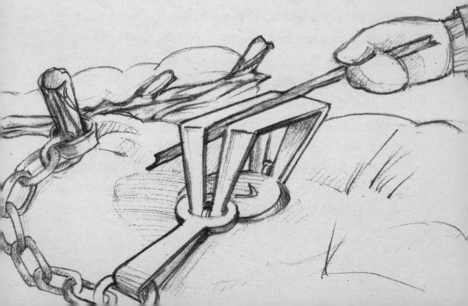

"Don't move," Chips warned, as he picked up a long stick from the ground.

Holding the stick in front of him, he reached down and started poking. With a vicious snap, the metal clamped shut, cutting the stick in half. It happened so fast I jumped back.

"What is it?" I wondered out loud.

"An animal trap." Chips's voice was angry. "Trappers set them to catch small game. They sell the furs."

"I'd sure hate to have one of those things snap shut on one of my legs," I said, shuddering.

"It's cruel," Chips agreed grimly. "I love animals. That's why I come out here looking for traps whenever I can. I spring as many as I find."

We followed the little stream and Chips found two more traps and tripped them. I was just about to ask him where the heck we were going when he turned into a trail that led up a steep hill.

When we reached the top, he stopped. "This is where I was standing when I saw it," he whispered, switching off the flashlight.

I looked out across a deep, wooded valley to where another, higher hill rose up. Chips just stood staring at that hill as if he were in a trance.

At first I thought the hill looked like all the others around us. And then I noticed that the trees seemed smaller, and there were more bushes. Also I could see huge boulders and piles of stones scattered about. What seemed to be an old, snow-covered road wound its way down the hill, appearing and disappearing through clumps of trees and behind boulders. It glowed like a ghostly river in the moonlight.

"Chips?" I asked gently. "What did you see over there that scared you?"

Chips shook his head as if he had forgotten I was there.

"I saw a werewolf," he answered.

6

"Werewolf?" I gasped. "Did you say werewolf?"

"I was out here last night looking for traps," Chips explained. "I had just found a few down below when suddenly I heard a man scream."

"Scream?" I gulped so hard that I must have looked like one of the fish in his aquarium.

"It sounded as if it came from somewhere above so I climbed up here to have a look around."

I had to give the kid credit. *I* would have run home.

"I saw this man," Chips went on as he pointed across the valley. "He was stumbling down that hill. About halfway, he stopped. Then suddenly . . . suddenly . . . he turned into a wolf!"

I wanted to say something but I felt as if the Pittsburgh Steelers were playing football in my mouth in their sweat socks.

"I mean it, Raymond," Chips said solemnly. "One

second this guy was standing there looking up at the moon—and the next he was gone and a wolf was standing there instead!"

"What did you do?" I asked, knowing what *I* would have done. Fainted!

"I just stood here looking over at it. I could see its evil eyes glowing red. And then it saw me! It ran down the hill and disappeared into the valley. I was too scared to move. I heard it crashing through the trees down there. And then, before I knew it, it was coming up *this* hill at me! I couldn't believe anything that big could move that fast. I knew it was going to kill me!"

"Didn't you run?" I asked fearfully.

"Sure I ran," Chips said, wiping tears from his eyes. "I ran back down the hill, but by the time I reached the bottom it was getting closer. I could hear it snapping and growling. I ran as fast as I could along the creek trail but I was afraid it was going to get me before I reached the footbridge. So I jumped in the water and started wading across. It was freezing cold but only up to my knees. I took a quick look over my shoulder and saw the werewolf just standing there at the edge of the creek, staring after me. I don't know why it didn't follow me through the water, but it didn't." Chips stopped for breath.

"Anyway," he finished, "when I got near the footbridge, I climbed out and started running again and I didn't look back.''

"I don't blame you," I said, glad the horrible tale was over. "And speaking of not looking back—let's go home.''

We were hurrying along the trail by the creek when Chips suddenly stopped in his tracks.

"Did you hear that?'' he whispered. "Something's coming.''

"Something?'' I squeaked.

Then I heard it too. Something *was* crashing loudly on the trail—ahead of us. Whatever creature it was, it let out a long, ghostly howl. The awful sound turned my legs to pudding.

"It's the werewolf!'' I shrieked.

Chips looked very calm, considering that we were standing there like so much dog chow. Or I should say, werewolf chow!

"It sounded more like a puppy with a toothache to me,'' he said.

I bit my lip and waited for the werewolf to come out of the trees. What emerged wasn't a monster, but it was almost as bad.

"Verna Wilkes!'' I yelled angrily. "What are you doing out here, scaring people half to death?''

"Just following you,'' she answered. "Anyone for a werewolf hunt?''

I thought back to the afternoon. Chips and I had talked under the big tree at school. Later I'd wondered where Verna had come from when she stepped on Bucky Bovine's foot. Now I knew. She had been hiding on the other side of the tree trunk, listening to everything.

"Forget it, Verna!" I cried. "Chips asked *me* to help him."

"Come off it, Raymond," Verna said with a nasty laugh. "If you were food, you would be a chicken nugget."

She was right, of course. I was beginning to understand why Chips had picked me, of all people, to tell his strange story to. It wasn't *my* help he was after.

"Verna's right," Chips confessed. "I want you to take my story to that friend of yours."

Anyone who reads the *Observer-Reporter* would know who Chips was talking about.

J. Huntley English, M.H.

7

Like many other people in the area, Chips had read how J. Huntley English, M.H., had solved what I call "The Case of the Horrible Swamp Monster" and "The Case of the Visiting Vampire." Chips had also read that I'd been involved in the cases and that Huntley and I were buddies. As we left Lost Woods, I agreed to visit Huntley the next day and tell him Chips's story.

Saturday I not only deliver my newspapers but I collect from my customers for the week. It was early afternoon by the time I finished, ate lunch, and headed over to Huntley's. I have to admit I felt better as I walked up the sidewalk to his house. If a werewolf really was wandering around Lost Woods, Huntley would know what to do. Why? Because the M.H. he adds after his name stands for Monster Hunter.

"Raymond Almond!" Mrs. English exclaimed as she let me in. "Where have you been hiding? Huntley is upstairs in his office. He'll be so glad to see you."

I should explain here why I hadn't seen Huntley in a long while, even though I consider him one of my best friends. Huntley is the same age as I am, but he goes to a special school for gifted kids in Pittsburgh. That's because he's super smart. He's not like anyone else I know. He's a loner who likes to be alone. If it weren't for the strange cases he had solved lately, very few people would even know he existed.

I walked up the stairs to Huntley's office. Because he's an only child, Mr. and Mrs. English let him use their third bedroom for his office. I stopped in front of the closed door and, as always, admired the sign.

J. HUNTLEY ENGLISH, M·H·
INVESTIGATOR
OF
UNEXPLAINED PHENOMENA

You see, Huntley firmly believes that real monsters do exist and, more than anything else, he wants to have a close encounter with one. His problem is that he lives in a small town in southwestern Pennsylvania. The closest thing we have to even a dinosaur is Bucky Bovine. But I have to give Huntley credit. He sure keeps trying.

I was just about to knock when an ear-splitting scream erupted from inside the room.

"Huntley?" I cried, throwing open the door. "Are you all right?"

Not only was Huntley all right, he looked downright relaxed. He was sitting in an overstuffed chair in front of his television set. I could see his video-cassette player was running. The scream had come from a movie he was watching.

"Raymond!" he cried happily. "You're just in time to see a new video cassette I bought."

"What is it?" I asked, pretty sure I didn't want to know.

"It is entitled 'I Wed a Werewolf from Weehawken.' "

I was right about not wanting to know.

"Well, turn it off because I just may have a case for you."

Huntley is as short and chunky as I am tall and skinny. But he can move mighty fast when he wants to. He jumped up, turned off the VCR, and sat down in the swivel chair behind his huge desk.

While he reached for his notepad and pen, I looked around the room. The walls are lined with monster-movie posters. The bookshelves are overflowing with science fiction and monster stories, as well as books on the supernatural. One whole corner is filled with

his horror-film video cassettes. A statue of Count Dracula stares at you from the desk and, to top it off, a dinosaur mobile hangs from the ceiling. Indiana Jones would love Huntley's office.

I sat down on one of the chairs facing the desk and waited for him to get settled.

"Now," he said, pushing his thick glasses up his nose. "I suppose this is about the werewolf that's wandering around Lost Woods."

8

"You know about it?" I cried in amazement and disappointment. I had wanted to be the one to tell him.

"I was informed this morning," Huntley answered.

"Did Verna tell you?"

"Verna Wilkes?" Huntley looked puzzled. "I haven't seen her since last fall."

"Then was it Tony Chipaletta?"

Huntley shook his head.

"I'm afraid I don't know him."

"Then who told you?"

"The identity of my source must remain confidential, Raymond."

"All right," I grumped. "But do you believe it? I mean, are werewolves for real?"

"Of course they are!" Huntley replied with gusto. "As long as there has been folklore, there have been tales of shape-shifting."

"Shape-shifting?"

"Shape-shifting means the ability to change shape. Usually the ability of a person to change into some kind of an animal. In mythology, the ancient Greek and Roman gods would disguise themselves as animals so they could walk among people without being noticed. Even before that, however, primitive peoples felt a close kinship with animals. Some tribes today still believe they share their souls with a certain animal. Since the beginning of time and folklore, there have been stories of shape-shifting from different cultures all around the world. Who am I to dispute that?"

"Then you do believe that there's a werewolf wandering around Lost Woods?"

Huntley shrugged his shoulders.

"I won't know for sure until I begin my investigation. Why don't you start by telling me how *you* heard about the werewolf."

I told him the story Chips had told me.

"That's similar to the story I heard this morning," Huntley said when I was finished. "Tonight I'd like you to take me out to the trailer park and introduce me to your friend Chips. After that, you and I will journey into the woods and begin our werewolf hunt."

"*Our* werewolf hunt?" I gulped. "Listen, Huntley, that thing attacked Chips the other night. I've heard the only way to kill a werewolf is by shooting it with

34

a silver bullet. Where are we going to get a gun and a silver bullet?''

Huntley shook his head.

''As I've said before, Raymond, my mission in life is to study monsters, not to destroy them.''

''But what if it attacks us?''

''Don't worry. I'm going to spend this afternoon studying my werewolf books for ways to protect us. Come back tonight after dinner and we'll head for Lost Woods.''

''All right,'' I said reluctantly, ''but I'd better warn you now. Verna Wilkes will be with me.''

Huntley's face fell when he heard this bit of news. Verna once had told Huntley that if he were food, he'd be a banana-nut fruitcake.

''What could I do?'' I said, throwing up my hands. ''She overheard Chips and me talking at school. Then she followed me out to Lost Woods last night and heard even more. She wants in and, if we don't let her, she'll just follow us. You know what Verna's like when she decides to be a pain.''

Huntley smiled. That's one of the things I like about him. He never stays down for long.

''Verna was a big help on my last two cases. I'd rather have her working with me than against me. I'll see you both tonight.''

I stepped into the hall and closed the office door

again. As I headed down the stairs, another scream tore through the house, followed by a voice shouting, "Werewolf! Werewolf! Help me, somebody! Please help me!"

This time I just smiled and kept on walking. Maybe Huntley was going to research werewolves this afternoon, but first he was going to finish that stupid movie.

9

Huntley has a different monster-hunting outfit for every season of the year. When he puts one of them on, you know he's ready to get down to serious monster business. As he, Verna, and I walked out the Washington Pike that night, he had on his winter gear. He was wearing this huge white imitation-fur coat. A red fur cap with built-in earmuffs was pushed down on his head. From the neck up, he looked like a Russian soldier. From the neck down, he looked like a snowball.

"This is just like old times!" Huntley sang merrily. "Heigh ho! Heigh ho! It's monster hunting we go!"

Huntley is never happier than when he's hot on the trail of a monster. I was glad he was having a good time. Above our heads, clouds had covered the moon, making the countryside extra dark. Before we reached the turn off to the trailer park, it had begun to snow.

"Great," Verna muttered, looking up into the flakes. "And I could be at the movies with my girl friends tonight."

"Don't forget, Verna," I snapped, "*you* invited yourself along on this expedition."

"And don't *you* forget, Raymond," she snapped back, "I saved your miserable life in Lost Swamp last year when you thought a monster was about to get you."

No one can shut me up quite like Verna can. She was telling the truth, all right. And I had to admit to myself that I *was* glad she was along. Verna's plenty tough. If she were food, she would be beef jerky. If I had to face a werewolf, I wanted Verna and Huntley by my side. Or better yet, in front of me!

We arrived at the Chipaletta trailer and found Chips in his room changing the filter in his aquarium. After being introduced, Huntley asked him to repeat his story. He did.

"Thank you," Huntley said when Chips was finished. "And now it's time for us to pierce the gloom of Lost Woods in search of our furry friend."

"I'll get my coat," Chips said.

"No." Huntley held up his hand. "You stay here. Werewolf tracking is a job for professional monster hunters. My esteemed colleagues and I will take this case from here."

"But I have to go out and look for traps," Chips protested.

"We'll do that for you," Huntley reassured him, as we left the warm trailer and stepped into the snowy night.

Chips looked relieved. I didn't blame him.

"Why couldn't he come along?" I asked as we passed the last trailer before the bridge. "We may need all the help we can get if that werewolf attacks us."

"A werewolf is one of the most dangerous monsters alive," Huntley said solemnly. "I can't take responsibility for a civilian like Chips when the going gets dangerous."

"What about a civilian like me?" I wanted to cry out, but I kept quiet.

I also didn't like the way Huntley had said "*when* the going gets dangerous." I would have preferred the word "if."

"Are we going to try to capture this werewolf or what?" Verna asked as we crossed the footbridge.

"Not tonight," Huntley answered, to my relief. "*First* we have to prove there really is a werewolf wandering around these woods. If there is, *then* we'll make plans to go after it."

It was snowing harder now and the woods were darker than ever. I led off along the narrow trail, shining

Huntley's flashlight into the swirling gloom. After a few minutes, I stopped at the point where Chips had sprung the first trap. I aimed the light along the edge of the water and soon spotted ugly metal jaws hidden in a snowbank.

"What is it?" Verna asked.

"Animal trap," Huntley answered.

He picked up a long stick from the ground and poked the end into the trap. Even Verna jumped when the vicious jaws snapped closed over the stick.

"How could anyone do that to a poor animal?" Verna asked angrily.

None of us had an answer to that as we found and set off three more of the cruel traps.

"Freeze!" Huntley suddenly whispered.

"I *am* freezing," Verna complained.

Now we all heard it.

"Quiet," Huntley hissed. "Someone's coming."

"Or something," I said with a shiver. "Like maybe a werewolf?"

10

"Run for it," somebody cried.

I'm pretty sure it was me.

"No," another voice cut in. "Hide."

I think that was Huntley.

We were almost at the place where Chips had led me away from the creek and up the hill to the lookout spot.

"Hide where?"

I'm pretty sure that was me again.

"Behind a tree, you dope! You're in a woods, you know."

That had to be Verna. Huntley would never call me a dope.

Each of us found a tree near the trail to crouch behind.

"Please let it be Chips," I silently prayed as the sounds got louder.

But I knew it couldn't be Chips. Whoever or whatever was approaching wasn't coming from the direction of the trailer park. Finally I couldn't stand it any more. I decided to face my fate and peered around the tree trunk. It wasn't a werewolf I saw sliding down the hillside toward the creek. It was Bucky Bovine!

I watched as Bucky knelt and picked up the last trap we had sprung. With an angry cry, he threw the trap down and moved on to the next one. After checking the fourth trap, he stomped off back up the hill. We waited until we couldn't hear him at all before leaving our hiding places.

"I might have guessed Bucky Bovine would be the one setting those awful traps," Verna fumed, as we started to climb what she named Lookout Hill.

"I bet that's why he got mad at me for talking to Chips the other day," I added. "He must have thought Chips was asking me to help him spring the traps."

Huntley was about to say something when we heard a noise that was sad and scary all at once. I will remember that sound if I live to be thirty years old. It was the long, shrill cry of a wolf!

"It came from the hill across the valley," I cried. "Where Chips first saw the werewolf."

"Lead on, Raymond!" Huntley said excitedly. "To the hunt!"

Raymond Almond, the Often Nervous, usually leads

the way to Majersky's Ice Cream Parlor. He does *not* lead the way at monster hunts! But this time there wasn't much choice. I led them to the top of the hill, where we stood and looked across the valley.

"See where that old road disappears into those trees about halfway up the hill?" I pointed. "That's where Chips saw the man change into the werewolf."

"Werewolf Hill!" Verna breathed. Even she sounded subdued.

Because of the falling snow and the clouds covering the moon, the hill was much darker than on the night before. There were no more howls. The only sound was the soft clicking of the icy snow as it brushed against the bare tree branches. The three of us stood

quietly and peered into the gloomy darkness.

Then, "Look!" Huntley whispered.

Verna leaned forward and squinted her eyes.

"Look at what?"

"I don't see anything either, Hunt," I said.

"There!" he hissed. "On the road."

I don't know about the other monster hunters, but I held my breath as I watched the dark outline of a figure moving through the snow. It stopped at the point where the road disappeared into the trees.

The wind swirled and threw a wave of snow into our faces. I blinked and then gasped at what I saw. The figure had disappeared and something else had appeared in its place.

"It's a werewolf!" Huntley cried excitedly. "It's a real honest-to-goodness, no-fooling-around, howling, growling werewolf!"

11

We watched in awe as the werewolf raised his huge head. I realized with a growing fear that he was sniffing the air. A few seconds later, he stared across the valley to where we were standing.

"I think he smells us," Verna said. "All right, Mr. Monster Hunter, what's your plan?"

"Yeah, Hunt," I piped up. "You told me yesterday you were going to study your books for ways to protect us from werewolves."

Huntley shrugged his shoulders sheepishly.

"I did. But I'm afraid I didn't find much useful information."

"What?" I squeaked.

"There seem to be as many suggestions for werewolf protection as there are cultures that believe in them," he explained. "None of the ones I found sounded as if they would work too well."

"You mean to tell me we're out here in the middle of nowhere with a werewolf on the loose and no protection?" Verna demanded.

"Well . . . not exactly," Huntley replied. "I did bring something."

He reached into his coat pocket and held out some small objects to us.

"Dog biscuits?" Verna yelled. "You brought dog biscuits to protect us from a werewolf?"

"Please keep an open mind, Verna," Huntley pleaded. "Mr. Amici, our mailman, told me he carries dog biscuits on his route and throws them to mean dogs."

"This isn't just a mean dog!" Verna shrieked. "This is a werewolf!"

"That's why I bought the jumbo size," Huntley replied. "Do you want one or not?"

"*I'll* take one," I said, grabbing a biscuit from his hand.

I looked across the valley to Werewolf Hill.

"Oh, my gosh!" I exclaimed. "Where did he go?"

"There he is!" Verna cried. "He's down in the valley. Coming here!"

"Coming fast!" I screamed.

"Monsters hunters, retreat!" Huntley yelled.

When it comes to running from danger, Raymond Almond, the Increasingly Nervous, *always* leads the way. That night was no exception as I ran back down the hill with Verna, Huntley, and the werewolf somewhere behind me. Like Chips Chipaletta, I'm a fast runner, especially when I'm being chased by a werewolf. But I was going *too* fast. I tripped over a tree root and went flying downward out of control. I ended up stuck headfirst in a snowbank beside the creek.

I screamed when something grabbed my leg. I thought it was the werewolf. Then something grabbed my other leg and pulled. Out I popped. Huntley and Verna had yanked me clear.

A terrible snarling, growling sound was approaching. The werewolf was almost upon us!

"The tree! Up that tree!" Huntley shouted.

Nearby was a tree with branches perfectly spaced for climbing. Huntley went first, with Verna right behind him, pushing his rear end up. I jumped onto the lowest limb but, before I could climb to the next one, the werewolf lunged up and grabbed the seat of my pants!

"It's got me!" I screamed, as I felt myself being pulled back down.

Verna and Huntley reached for me from above and yanked on my arms. As they hauled me up with a mighty tug, I heard something tearing. I hoped it wasn't my poor body.

While I was struggling for a secure grip on the

limb beside them, I suddenly felt very cold. At first I thought it was from fear. Then I realized that the werewolf had ripped my pants right off!

I was sitting in a tree in Lost Woods at night in a blizzard in my underwear!

When I dared look down, I saw the giant werewolf leaping angrily up at us. As high as we were, we were just barely out of reach of his terrible teeth.

The sight of those savage jaws snapping open and shut like the steel traps we had just sprung made us hold our dangling feet as high as we could.

"Hey, Raymond!" Verna suddenly said with a grin. "Nice legs!"

12

"I'm hungry," Verna groaned.

"I'm cold," I shivered.

"I'm amazed!" Huntley exclaimed. "Imagine! I've been run up a tree by a real live werewolf!"

He made it sound as if our predicament were a big honor or something. For about fifteen minutes, the werewolf had been lunging violently up at us. Now it sat on the ground with its huge tongue hanging out, looking up with its evil eyes.

"So what are we going to do?" I asked.

"Wait for it to go away," Huntley answered.

"I'm hungry," Verna moaned again.

"What if it doesn't go away?" I persisted.

"We'll wait up here until morning," Huntley explained. "When the sun comes up, the werewolf will turn back into a human being again. I'd love to see that!"

"That's because you have pants on," I grumped.

Verna stared down at the werewolf. "Give me your dog biscuit, Raymond," she said.

We all stared down at the werewolf. He stared up at us.

Crunch!

I looked over at Verna. She was munching on the dog biscuit I had handed her.

"This isn't too bad," she said between chews. "Sort of tastes like one of my mother's brownies."

I made a mental note not to eat any of Mrs. Wilkes's brownies if they were ever offered to me.

I looked back down at the werewolf. Suddenly he cocked his head as if listening to something. I couldn't hear anything above the wind and my chattering teeth. But the werewolf jumped up on all four feet and bounded off in the direction from which he had come.

"D-d-do you think he's gone?" I chattered.

"Why don't you climb down and see?" Verna suggested helpfully.

"I'll go," Huntley said stoutly. "I'm the leader of this expedition."

"Be c-c-c-careful," I stammered between shivers.

Huntley began to lower himself to the next limb.

"He may be weird but he sure has guts," Verna said.

We watched as Huntley reached the ground.

51

"I think he's gone," Huntley called up to us. "Hurry!"

He didn't have to say it twice. We quickly climbed down, and the three of us left Lost Woods as fast as we could. It was getting late so we hurried through the trailer park and back out onto the Washington Pike.

"So what's next?" Verna asked the Monster Hunter.

"Now I must gather enough evidence to prove to the scientific community that our friend back there is a real werewolf."

I couldn't figure out what scientific community Huntley was talking about. The only scientist in Barkley was old Professor Swick, who once accidentally blew up his toolshed during an experiment.

I was about to ask when a car full of high-school girls slowed down beside us. Opening the windows, the girls began whistling and clapping.

Quickly I took off my coat and wrapped it around my waist. A sex symbol I'm not!

13

Huntley and Verna decided to stop at Majersky's Ice Cream Parlor for sundaes. I headed straight home. Since Mr. Majersky once threw a kid out of his store for coming in without shoes, I didn't think he'd be too thrilled to see me coming in without pants. Luckily Mom and Dad were in the kitchen talking when I got home, so I was able to sneak down the hall to my bedroom without having to explain my undressed state.

After church and Sunday dinner the next day, I watched the Steelers get trounced by the Chicago Bears on television. Since that depressed me, I decided to walk over to Huntley's house. He's always so glad to see me that I usually get cheered up real fast.

I was just about to knock on the door of his office when once again a scream erupted from inside. This time I didn't panic as I opened the door. I knew he was at his VCR again.

"Oh, no!" I exclaimed as I shut the door behind me. "Not 'I Wed A Werewolf From Wisconsin' again?"

"It's 'I Wed A Werewolf From Weehawken,' " Huntley corrected me, "and it's a fine film. Pull up a chair. It's almost over."

That's one thing about Huntley. When he likes a monster movie, he can watch it over and over again without getting tired of it.

"No, thanks," I said. "I saw the *real* thing last night. Remember?"

I went over to one of his bookshelves and gathered up his books on werewolves. Someone in the movie was screaming, "He's turning into a werewolf! Run! Run!" I spread the books out on Huntley's desk and tried to concentrate.

I quickly found that what Huntley had said last night was true. There *were* lots of suggestions from around the world on how to protect yourself from werewolves. In Italy they believed that little wax crosses would do the job. In Ireland and Scotland they thought you might protect yourself with the branch of a yew tree, a piece of mistletoe, or an ash twig. In someplace called Messina they were sure you could bring a werewolf out of its spell by hitting it with a specially shaped key. The dumbest suggestion came from Denmark. They felt that all you had to do was walk up to the werewolf and say something like, "Gee, I think it's awful you're a werewolf," and the werewolf would change back into a person again. Sure! After reading those suggestions, Huntley's dog biscuits didn't seem so dumb after all. At least they'd given Verna something to eat.

When the movie was over, Huntley switched off the VCR and TV and stood looking out the window. It was a beautiful winter's day. The late afternoon sun held its own in a cloudless blue sky. It was hard to believe that last night we had faced a werewolf in a blizzard.

"Do you feel like a walk, Raymond?" Huntley asked as I put the werewolf books back on the shelf.

"Lost Woods, right?" I said with a sinking heart.

Huntley smiled.

"That seems to be where the action is these days."

"Sure, why not?" I answered, trying to smile back. "A day without a werewolf is like a day without sunshine."

Huntley pulled two leather carrying cases from the closet. One contained a camera, the other a portable tape recorder. After we bundled up, he handed me the tape recorder to carry.

"Do you think Verna will want to come?" he asked. "She's in on this, too."

"Are you kidding? You can't pry Verna away from

the television on Sunday until every football game in the country is over with.''

As we walked up the street, I felt extra glad that everything looked bright and cheerful and normal. The yards were filled with kids building snowmen and having snowball fights. I just didn't like the idea of going monster hunting without Verna, though. I would never let her know that she always makes things seem less scary. But, as long as I had to venture into Lost Woods without her, I was glad it was on such a sunny day.

I had forgotten just how fast it gets dark in winter.

"I want to explore Werewolf Hill," Huntley explained as we walked out the Washington Pike.

We were at the turn-off to the Locust Grove Trailer Park. I was surprised when Huntley kept on walking along the Pike.

"Where are we going?" I asked.

"Let's see if we can find a different way to that hill," he suggested. "The old road that runs down it must come out of Lost Woods somewhere."

"It sure ought to be easier," I agreed. "Trying to climb that slope from the valley would be tough. Especially after the extra snow that fell last night."

Our walk that afternoon was quiet and lonely, though I had to admit that the fresh snow made Lost Woods look almost beautiful. I had to remind myself that a dangerous monster had attacked us somewhere in there.

Huntley seemed lost in heavy monster-hunting

thoughts. The only sound was an occasional avalanche of snow falling from a tree limb to the ground. I started to do some thinking on my own. Last night we had seen what looked like a person turning into a werewolf. And yet we had seen only one other person in Lost Woods besides us. Bucky Bovine. Could that have been Bucky we had seen on Werewolf Hill?

"This might be it." Huntley's voice interrupted my thoughts.

I looked ahead to the left and saw a break in the trees where a narrow road emerged from the woods onto the highway.

"We don't know if that's the right road or not," I commented.

"And we won't know unless we try it," Huntley said. "Come on. It gets dark early these days."

We followed the old road into the woods. It ran in a straight line for a quarter of a mile or so.

"Too bad it snowed last night," Huntley commented. "Any important tracks have been covered over."

We walked around a large snowdrift where the road emerged into a clearing. Beyond the clearing, the road crossed a rickety old iron bridge that spanned a creek.

"It doesn't look too safe," I said, studying the bridge. "Think it will hold us?"

"We'll cross one at a time," Huntley soothed.

We did and then followed the road deeper into the trees. For about half a mile it wound its way among the silent, wooded hills. I was just beginning to wonder if this was the road we wanted when it finally turned and began to wind its way up a hill. Our hike was tougher now because the slope of the road made it more slippery. When we finally reached the top, we were both out of breath.

"How do we know this is the right hill?" I asked as we took a brief rest. "It looks like all the others around here."

"It's Werewolf Hill all right," Huntley declared. "See how most of the trees on this hill are smaller than the trees on the other hills? I noticed that last night, though it was hard to see in the storm. And look at the boulders and piles of stones scattered around."

But I wasn't looking at any of that stuff now. I was looking nervously at the sky. It was getting very dark, very fast. The moon, which was getting fuller, had even appeared.

"What do we do now?" I asked anxiously.

"Let's follow the road down the hill," Huntley suggested. "If we can find the spot where we saw the figure turn into the werewolf, we can look for clues there."

We had just started down the slope when Huntley stopped suddenly and held up a warning hand.

"What's the matter?" I whispered nervously.

"I think I heard someone cough back there," Huntley answered. "Quick! Hide!"

Huntley ran toward the nearest boulder but I beat him to it. When it comes to hiding, no one is faster than I am! We crouched behind the big rock and peered over the top. A figure was coming down the hill toward us. Now I was glad for the thickening darkness. Whoever was coming might not notice our footprints in the snow.

I held my breath as the figure walked by our hiding place. I almost choked when I saw that it was someone I knew.

Swallowing hard, I watched Bucky Bovine walk on down the road to where it disappeared in a grove of trees.

15

"What's he doing here?" I whispered.

"Quick!" Huntley said. "Hand me the tape recorder!"

I watched as he pulled the recorder out of its carrying case. Since there was already a cassette inside, he just hit the record button.

We waited behind the boulder. For a long while the only sound was the hum of the tape recorder. And then a terrifying scream rose from below.

"Oh, no! Oh, no! I'm turning into a werewolf!"

"I think that's B-B-B-Bucky!" I chattered.

"Come on," Huntley said, pulling his camera out of its case. "I want to go down there and get some pictures."

"Forget it!" I cried. "Let's get out of here!"

"But, Raymond," Huntley protested. "This could be history in the making."

"It could also be pain in the making!" I whined.

I picked up the tape recorder and began running up the hill. Let Huntley stay and pretend like he was filming a National Geographic Special.

"Raymond! Wait up!"

I looked around and saw Huntley running through the snow after me. With that dumb white fur coat he was wearing, he looked like the Son of the Abominable Snowman.

"I thought you were going to take some pictures?" I said, when he reached me.

"I forgot to bring my flash attachment," he replied, catching his breath. "It's too dark to take pictures without it."

Suddenly, from down the hill behind us, we heard the long, sad howl of a wolf. The sound made me shiver despite all the warm clothes I was wearing.

"Let's get going," I urged, "before Bucky smells us and trees us again. One trip home without my pants is enough."

Huntley didn't argue this time. We left the woods and got back into town a lot faster than we had come out. That's because I insisted we run.

Huntley's office never looked so good! He sat behind his desk while I sat in a chair rubbing my frozen feet through my socks. I watched him setting up his tape recorder.

After pushing the play button, he leaned back to listen. The cassette turned for awhile before the scream blasted from the speaker. Even though I knew it was coming, I jumped. Then we listened to that terrifying voice we had heard on the hill: "Oh, no! Oh, no! I'm turning into a werewolf!"

The next voice was mine, urging Huntley to run for it. I sounded so scared that even I felt embarrassed. Huntley rewound the tape and played it again. And again and again and again. Hearing it once was enough for me, but I sat patiently until Huntley put the recorder aside.

"Do you think Bucky Bovine's the werewolf?" I asked.

"The evidence is pointing that way," was the Monster Hunter's answer. "Chips said he saw a man change into a werewolf. Bucky's a big kid. From a distance, he *could* easily look like a man."

"And don't forget last night," I added, "when *we* saw the werewolf. We know Bucky was in the area."

Huntley nodded.

"And then there's the evidence we gathered tonight."

At that point, Huntley's Creature-from-the-Black-Lagoon clock on the wall chimed eight. It looks like a regular cuckoo clock. But Huntley had taken the little bird out of the inside. In its place, he'd glued a small model of the Creature from the Black Lagoon. Every hour when the clock chimes, this monster pops out at you.

"I have to get going," I said.

As I walked to the door, I stopped and picked up the camera case, which was sitting on the floor. Opening it up, I saw the flash attachment inside where it belonged.

I looked back at Huntley and smiled.

"The only reason you came after me back there was because you were worried about me. Thanks."

Huntley returned my smile.

"A smart Monster Hunter knows when to investigate and when to retreat. I think you had the right idea tonight, Raymond. It was getting dark, and Verna wasn't with us, and there I was about to take us down into unknown territory. It is I who thank you."

Good old Huntley!

16

"Bucky Bovine is the werewolf?" Verna's mouth popped open even wider than usual.

We were at school the next day and I was telling her about what Huntley and I had seen and heard the night before.

"*The* Bucky Bovine? *Our* Bucky Bovine?"

"It seems so," I answered.

"I know Bucky looks like Godzilla but—a were-wolf?"

The bell rang for first period so we split up, with Verna's mouth still hanging open like a black hole.

It wasn't easy concentrating on schoolwork that day. I kept looking around at my classmates, wondering what they would do if we announced that a werewolf was wandering the hallowed halls of our little school.

After dinner that night, Verna and I met Huntley at Majersky's Ice Cream Parlor. We found him in his favorite booth in the back, with his nose in a book.

"What are you reading?" I asked.

Huntley looked up in surprise.

"*Uh?* Oh, hello, Raymond. Verna. Please sit down."

As we slid into the booth, I could see by the cover that it was one of his werewolf books.

"Learning anything?" I asked.

Huntley finished his vanilla ice cream soda before answering.

"It says here that the Irish and Scots believe you can save yourself from a werewolf by getting on the other side of a running stream. They believe that werewolves can't cross water."

The waitress came and took our orders. Verna wanted a banana split. I had my usual, which is a chocolate soda with strawberry ice cream. This time Huntley ordered a hot fudge sundae.

"A monster hunter needs all the energy he can get," he explained.

"You get much more energy and you'll be bigger

than the monsters you're always chasing," Verna said with a snicker.

Our treats arrived, and for the next few minutes the only sound coming from our booth was slurping.

"What now, Hunt?" I asked, as we finished up.

"To the library. I want to look at a topographical map of the Lost Woods area."

"What's a topographical map?"

"It's a map that shows where things like hills and streams are," Verna explained, rather snootily.

"Details of the terrain," Huntley added.

It took us only a few minutes to get to the public library. Heck, it only takes a few minutes to get anywhere in Barkley.

We were glad to find Mr. Stevenson on duty at the reference desk. He's a friendly man who likes to help us kids find what we want. He showed us where the case filled with topographical maps was. And then he left us there to use them without even warning us to be careful.

Huntley found the map he wanted and spread it out on a desk. It showed the area in and around Lost Woods.

"Just as I thought," he said. "See? Lost Woods is completely surrounded by creeks."

"So?" Verna asked.

"The book I was just reading said that werewolves can't cross running water. Remember what Chips told us? When the werewolf was chasing him, Chips waded across the creek."

"And the werewolf didn't follow him over!" I said with a snap of my fingers. "It can't cross running water so it had to stop at the bank and let Chips get away."

"*Uh-oh!*" Verna cried. "Did you hear the weather report for the next week?"

"What about it?" I asked.

"The weatherman said we're in for a real cold spell with temperatures below zero."

"So? Wear long johns."

And then I understood what Verna was getting at.

"Oh, my gosh!" I said. "If we have a bad cold spell, all the creeks will freeze up. Then there won't be any running water to keep Bucky trapped in Lost Woods when he turns into a werewolf?"

"No one will be safe for miles around," Huntley added grimly.

17

Before going to sleep that night, I tuned my radio to WJPA for a weather update. The announcer confirmed Verna's report. The Pittsburgh area was in for a bitter cold spell.

I lay in the dark shivering, and not because it was going to be getting colder. The creeks I had seen in Lost Woods weren't very deep. It wouldn't take long for them to freeze up. So, if flowing creeks were the only things keeping the werewolf trapped in Lost Woods, we had to do something quick.

But what *could* we do? Kill the werewolf? I knew Huntley would never go for that. I wouldn't either. I really didn't know Bucky Bovine very well. Until the afternoon when he threatened to turn me into a sandwich spread, the worst thing he had ever done to me was to pretend I didn't exist. Maybe we could tell our story to Police Chief Murphy? No, I could hear the chief laughing already. Could we somehow capture the werewolf? But how?

I had too many questions and no answers as I fell asleep. That night I dreamed that I was invited to Verna's house for a birthday party. For refreshments, Mrs. Wilkes served dog biscuits. The jumbo kind. Verna's present from her parents was inside this big box. When she opened it, a werewolf jumped out.

The next day at school I saw Bucky in the hall. Usually he hangs out with guys from the football team. That morning he just stood by himself, looking glum. He looked the same way after school when I saw him walking toward the buses. I could understand that. Being a werewolf must be enough to depress anyone.

All at once I decided to do a little investigating on my own. Maybe it was because Bucky seemed so subdued that I decided to follow him. I grabbed Dave Price by the arm as he walked by. Dave's a friend of mine and he knows my paper route. I asked him if he would deliver the *Observer-Reporter* for me and he said, "No problem." That taken care of, I hopped on Bucky's bus.

I kept my head lowered as I started down the aisle. I figured a guy like Bucky would sit in the back seat. I dared a peek and, sure enough, I saw him all alone back there. I was glad to see that he was staring out the window and not at me. The front of the bus was crowded, but halfway back I found a space next to Chips Chipaletta.

"Raymond?" he asked in surprise. "What are you doing here?"

"*Shhhhhhhh,*" I whispered. "I'm working undercover, following Bucky Bovine."

"Hey, Raymond!" a voice from behind shouted. "What are you doing on our bus?"

So much for undercover. The voice belonged to a kid from my homeroom.

"He's going home with me," Chips called back.

"Thanks," I said to Chips.

I scrunched low in my seat, afraid that Bucky would catch on that I was following him. But he was apparently too wrapped up in his own problems to notice what was going on around him. I was safe, at least for the moment.

"Where does Bucky get off the bus?" I asked Chips.

"At Number Nine," he answered. "It's the next stop after mine."

"Do a lot of kids get off there?"

"Yeah. You should be able to blend in with the crowd."

The bus headed out the Washington Pike. I filled Chips in about the latest doings on Werewolf Hill until it stopped at the road leading down to the Locust Grove Trailer Park.

71

"Good luck, whatever you're up to," Chips said, as he joined the line of kids leaving the bus.

I didn't know what I was up to, exactly. I just thought if I could find out more about Bucky, it might help Huntley figure out what we were going to do about him.

Thick dark woods lined the Pike as we continued on. There were still a lot of kids on the bus, but I stayed low in my seat to be on the safe side. After a few more minutes, the bus stopped at the little village known as Number 9. Most of the remaining kids got up and crowded the aisle. I quickly got into the middle of them.

Once outside the kids began to scatter, so I looked for a place to hide. I chose a nearby tree and stepped behind it.

Bucky was the last to get off the bus. He still looked as if he had a terrible case of the blues as he walked up the street. Unsure of what to do next, I watched him moving away. My Sherlock Holmes plan didn't seem like such a good one any more. I was in a place I had never been before, with a long cold walk back to town. Probably in the dark. Worse still, I was on Bucky's home turf.

I was pretty sure I could outrun Bucky the Defensive Tackle. But Bucky the Werewolf was something else!

18

The village of Number 9 is mostly made up of two-story wooden houses lining both sides of the road. All of the houses look exactly alike. That's because Number 9 was a "company town." Years before, a mining company built the houses for the miners who worked for it. The name Number 9 comes from the fact that the miners who lived there worked in the Number 9 mine. The mine shut down long ago but the name stuck. There are a few old company towns in our area.

I followed Bucky down the street until he turned up the sidewalk at the last house at the end of the row.

I waited while he disappeared around the side of the house. Then I took a deep breath for nerve and followed him. I crept to the corner of the house and stopped. Then I peeked out back.

I was amazed to see that the yard was filled with pens and cages of all sizes and shapes. Rabbits, ducks, raccoons, and even a small fox were just some of the animals in this little zoo. I watched as Bucky went to work cleaning the pens and cages and bringing fresh straw from a shed at the end of the yard. After that, he began to give food and fresh water to all the animals. As he worked, he talked softly to the creatures. Some he took out of their cages and gently held.

"Bucky?" I heard a voice call from the back porch.

"Yeah, Ma?" Bucky answered.

"Someone dropped off a kitten he found down near the creek. It was half frozen and starved. I have it in here in a box near the stove."

"Be right in, Ma."

"How's the fox doing?" Mrs. Bovine asked.

74

Bucky put food into the pen that held the little fox. That's when I noticed the animal had a slight limp as it walked over to its dish.

"It's doing better, Ma. A few more weeks and it will be good as new. Then I can set it free in the woods where it belongs."

"I declare, Bucky," Mrs. Bovine said with a laugh. "If you don't become a veterinarian when you grow up, you'll have missed your true calling."

Bucky finished his chores and went into the house. I stood on tiptoes and peeked in the kitchen window.

I watched as Bucky leaned over a box next to the stove and picked up the smallest kitten I had ever seen. Mrs. Bovine poured some milk from a saucepan into a little bottle and handed it to her son. Bucky fed the kitten as tenderly as if it were a baby.

I snuck back along the side of the house to the street. As I started the long, cold walk back to town, I was beginning to feel very foolish. Here I had come all this way to investigate Bucky, and what had I found out? That he loved animals. Big deal!

The village of Number 9 sits on the edge of Lost Woods. Darkness was falling quickly so I tried to concentrate on Bucky to keep from thinking how spooky it was getting as I jogged along by myself. The wild woods grew right to the edge of the highway and made my walk even darker and more lonely.

Soon I was passing the spot where the abandoned road came out of the woods and joined the Pike. It seemed so long ago that Huntley and I had left the woods on that old road after learning the truth about Bucky. As I hurried past, an awful roaring sound exploded out of the darkness. I jumped behind the nearest tree and waited for whatever was making the sound to eat me.

I was relieved to see a truck and not a monster coming toward me out of the old road. I watched as it pulled out onto the highway. Then it sped off toward town. Not until it was on its way up the Pike did the driver bother to turn on the lights.

It wasn't until I was home that I stopped to think what a dangerous way that was to drive.

19

The next night after dinner I walked over to Huntley's house. I couldn't believe what I saw when I stepped into his office. He was sitting in front of his TV watching that dumb movie again!

"Not 'I Wed a Werewolf from Washington' again?" I cried.

"Not Washington, Raymond. Weehawken. It's a city in New Jersey. Let me show you where it is on the map."

"Forget it," I said, walking over to the VCR.

A man on the screen was screaming "Oh, no! Oh, no! I'm turning into a were——" I cut the man off in mid-scream by turning the VCR off.

"There's something about that movie," Huntley said, more to himself than to me, as he got up and sat behind his desk.

I quickly told him what I had found out about Bucky

Bovine the day before. It wasn't much, but I figured since I had gone to all that trouble I might as well share my findings. Besides, Huntley says that all facts are important in a case.

I was just finishing my report when the office door suddenly flew open with a bang. When I saw who was standing there, I jumped to my feet in shock. It was Bucky Bovine, and he looked plenty mad!

All I could think of was that he had found out I'd followed him. I tried to remind myself that this was someone who nurses sick kittens. But then I remembered that it was also someone who terrorizes opposing quarterbacks.

But Bucky stomped by me and leaned over Huntley's desk.

"Now you listen to me, English," he growled, "and you listen good! I don't want you and your friends snooping around Lost Woods again! Understand?"

"I think we need to talk about this, Bucky," Huntley answered calmly.

"You just do what I say or your monster-hunting days are over!"

With that Bucky spun around, shoved me back down into my chair, and stomped out of the room as fast as he had come in.

Huntley sat quietly for a moment, as if deep in thought.

"Bucky's scared," he finally said.

"Scared?" I repeated, rubbing my sore chest. "He didn't look scared to me. He looked mad."

"That's how someone like Bucky reacts to fear. He's afraid, all right. We have to do something to help him. And we have to do it soon, before it's too late."

"But what can we do?" I asked.

Huntley thought about it for a moment.

"I'm not sure yet. I am sure that Bucky doesn't like changing into a werewolf. He can't control it. That's why he goes deep into Lost Woods when he feels a spell coming on. He knows he can't escape from the woods and hurt anyone as long as the creeks around the woods are flowing."

"And somehow he's found out we're investigating him," I added. "He's afraid we'll be in Lost Woods some night when he turns into a werewolf and he'll attack us. He doesn't want us out there because, in his own way, he's trying to protect us."

"Exactly," Huntley agreed.

"But why doesn't he just ask you to help him?"

"He's probably seen those movies that always end with the werewolf's being killed. He doesn't trust me, and I can't say I blame him."

Suddenly I felt something I never thought I would ever feel. I felt sorry for Bucky.

"Bucky knows as well as we do that it's going to be getting colder," Huntley went on. "The creeks around Lost Woods will freeze. And then there will be nothing to keep him from leaving the woods and stalking human prey. And when people find out there's a monster in their midst, they'll soon be stalking him."

"We've got to help him!" I cried.

"We will," Huntley said grimly. "We will."

20

Huntley called a meeting in his office the next night after dinner. We quickly brought Verna up to date.

"So what are we going to do?" she demanded.

Verna always likes to get right to the point.

"Bucky's afraid," Huntley explained, "and he's not going to *let* us help him. So we're going to have to trap him and hold him so he can't hurt anybody and so nobody can hurt him."

"And then what?" Verna asked.

"We bring Police Chief Murphy to see him. When the chief watches Bucky turn into a werewolf, he'll have to believe us. Then maybe he can get doctors and scientists to come and try to find a cure for Bucky."

"So we're going to try and trap Bucky *before* he turns into a werewolf?" I asked fearfully.

I figured it would take nothing less than a squad of Marines to get the drop on Bucky Bovine.

Huntley shrugged his shoulders.

"I'd rather face Bucky as a human being than Bucky as a werewolf."

I saw his point, although it didn't make me feel much better.

"When and how do we do this?" Verna asked.

"Friday night," Huntley answered. "I've checked the Farmer's Almanac. The moon will be full then. I'm pretty sure that Bucky will go into Lost Woods that night to turn into a werewolf. We'll be waiting to trap him."

Lost Woods at night again! I sure didn't like the sound of that. And tomorrow was Friday!

"Maybe we should wait for the *next* full moon?" I suggested hopefully.

"Sorry, Raymond," Huntley answered. "All the creeks will surely be frozen by tomorrow night. We have to act quickly."

"You've only answered half my question," Verna persisted. "Now I know *when*. But tell me *how* we're going to trap Bucky for Chief Murphy to come and watch."

"I haven't figured that out yet," Huntley admitted.

"Just so whatever you figure out doesn't include dog biscuits," Verna muttered.

"Let's go to Majersky's," Huntley said, cheerful at the mention of food. "I always think better after a double chocolate malted."

We headed down to Barkley's shopping district. As we walked along Main Street, we stopped to check out the video cassettes on display in the window of the Barkley Video. It's the store where Huntley rents and buys most of his monster videos. Inside we could see Mr. Hughey, the owner, standing behind the counter, unpacking some boxes. When he looked up, we waved. He waved back and motioned us into the store.

There was only one other customer there. A tall man wearing jeans and a ski jacket was browsing near the counter. We walked past him toward Mr. Hughey.

"Hi, kids!" Mr. Hughey greeted us. "I've just gotten a shipment of new videos and there's one in particular I think will interest you."

Mr. Hughey pulled a video cassette out of a box and handed it to Huntley.

"My distributor says I'm the very first in the area to get this," Mr. Hughey exclaimed happily.

I looked over Huntley's shoulder at the title and couldn't help groaning. It was "I Wed a Werewolf from Weehawken."

Huntley shook his head.

"I'm sorry, Mr. Hughey, but I already have a copy of this."

"What?" Mr. Hughey asked in surprise. "Where did you get it?"

"I bought it down the street at Barney Beeker's Bargain Emporium a few weeks ago. It only cost me ten dollars."

"Ten dollars?" Mr. Hughey cried. "Why, I'll have to sell mine for at least twenty-five just to make a small profit. I don't understand this!"

As we left the store, Mr. Hughey was still muttering angrily to himself.

21

"All right, Mr. Monster Hunter," Verna said as Huntley sucked air noisily through his straw. "You've had your malted. Now tell us your plan."

Huntley pushed his glass away and then stared at it as if another malted would magically appear any minute. I know Huntley when he gets that faraway look in his eyes, and I knew he *hadn't* heard a word she had said.

"Well?" Verna demanded.

"Quiet," I hissed. "He's thinking."

Huntley went on thinking for several minutes while Verna mumbled terrible things under her breath. I couldn't really blame her. In twenty-four hours we would be in the heart of Lost Woods trying to capture poor Bucky before he could change into a werewolf. We needed a plan and we needed one soon.

"I'm going to the library," Huntley suddenly announced. "Meet me at Shorty's at five o'clock for dinner tomorrow. After we eat, I'll tell you my plan and we'll embark on our monster mission. Be sure to dress warmly."

With that he hurried out the door.

"I'm telling you," Verna said, tapping her forehead with her finger. "That boy is missing a few screws in his tool chest."

I looked up and spotted Mrs. Pisarcik, our waitress, coming over with the check. Verna hadn't seen her yet.

"Well," I said, looking at my watch and standing up. "I'd better get going, too. See you tomorrow, Verna."

Before I stepped out the door, I looked back in time to see Mrs. Pisarcik presenting Verna with our check. I could almost see the smoke coming out of Verna's ears.

I hurried down Main Street in case Verna decided to chase me. I didn't slow down until I reached the lighted window of Barney Beeker's Bargain Emporium. When I looked inside, I noticed that Mr. Hughey from Barkley Video was there talking to Mr. Beeker, who owns the Emporium. Yelling is a better word, because Mr. Hughey looked plenty mad. He was standing on one side of a bin filled with video cassettes. Mr. Beeker was standing on the other side of the bin, yelling back.

Now Mr. Hughey was waving a video cassette angrily in the air. Somehow I *knew* it was "I Wed a Werewolf from Weehawken."

"Raymond!" I heard a voice down the street screaming. "You owe me a dollar and seventy-five cents! Plus tax!"

I quickly turned away from the window and crashed into someone. I looked up and saw that it was the tall man who had been browsing in Mr. Hughey's video store earlier.

"I'm sorry," I apologized.

The man didn't answer, so I figured he wasn't mad. Half a block down the street, I looked back. He was still standing at the window, peering in at the argument.

22

Shorty's is a small restaurant on Chestnut Street. It specializes in hot dogs smothered with onions, mustard, and chili sauce. As we sat at the counter the next night, wolfing down our dogs, I couldn't help wondering if I were eating my last meal.

Verna was still mad about getting stuck with the check at Majersky's the night before. Huntley assured her that tonight's meal was his treat.

"Monster Hunters!" Huntley announced as he paid the bill. "To the hunt! The werewolf hunt, that is!"

We began bundling up. Huntley, of course, was wearing his furry winter monster-hunting outfit.

"It sure gets dark early this time of year," I said, as we stepped outside and began walking toward the outskirts of town.

It was a clear but very cold night. Already the sky was filled with stars. But it wasn't the stars or the cold that made me shiver. It was the huge moon rising over the hills. The moon that would soon be turning poor Bucky Bovine into a raging, awesome werewolf.

"This is going to be a dangerous mission." Huntley began filling us in as we stepped out on the Washington Pike. "One of us in particular will have to do something very brave."

I felt a little better when I heard that, because I knew he couldn't be talking about me. The name Raymond Almond and the word "brave" have never been used in the same sentence.

"As we've deduced, when Bucky knows he's going to turn into a werewolf," Huntley went on, "he goes to the middle of Lost Woods where he can be alone and no one will see him."

"And where he can't hurt anybody once he's changed," I added.

Huntley nodded.

"He seems to go to the same hill, so that's where we'll be waiting for him tonight."

"And?" Verna urged.

"And we capture him *before* he can change into a werewolf."

"We're going to jump him, right?" Verna asked.

"Too dangerous," Huntley answered. "We're going to try and trap him in the shack."

"What shack?" I asked.

"The shack near the entrance to the mine shaft," Huntley answered.

"What mine shaft?" Verna asked.

"The mine shaft that goes down into the hill."

"How do you know there's a mine shaft there?" I asked.

"I kept wondering about the trees on that hill. Remember how they're smaller than the other trees growing in the woods? Why? All I could figure was that the trees on that hill were once cut down and they haven't had time to grow back as tall as the other trees. Everyone knows that there are old abandoned mine shafts all over Lost Woods. So I guessed that—"

"—a mining company cut the trees down a long time ago," I finished for him. "And so, there must be a mine shaft there somewhere."

"Right. And then there was that old abandoned road. Why would there be a road connecting that part of the woods to the highway?"

"The mining company built the road to haul the coal out," Verna answered.

"That's what I figured. So I went back to the library last night and looked at that map of Lost Woods more closely. And sure enough, it shows a mine entrance part way down that hill. After that, Mr. Stevenson helped me find a book called *A History of Coal Mining*

90

in Washington County. It was most interesting! There was even a picture of *that* particular mine! The picture showed the mine entrance with a small building nearby. They probably used the building for the supervisor's office and first aid station.''

Just ahead I could see the road that connected the Locust Grove Trailer Park with the Pike.

"That mine has been abandoned for a long time," Verna pointed out. "How can you be sure the shack is still standing?"

"A good monster hunter must have faith, Verna," Huntley said solemnly.

His answer didn't reassure me much, but I didn't have time to worry about it. A crashing sound to our left stopped us dead. Any second I expected the were-wolf to come lunging out of the woods at us!

23

But it wasn't a werewolf that emerged from the woods beside the Pike. It was a human figure. For a second I thought it might be Bucky Bovine and I almost bit my tongue. But as the figure walked closer, my fear turned to surprise and relief.

"Chips?" I cried.

Chips Chipaletta walked up to us and smiled.

"I hope I'm not late, Huntley? I was looking for traps."

"You're right on time," Huntley answered. "Do you remember the instructions I gave you over the phone?"

"Sure do. You want me stationed on the hill where I was when I first saw the werewolf. You'll be up on Werewolf Hill watching for Bucky. After you trap him, you'll blink your flashlight three times in my direction. When I see your signal, I'll know it's time for me to run and phone Police Chief Murphy and lead him to you.''

"Correct,'' Huntley said. "Then the chief can watch Bucky turn into a werewolf.''

"And what if Bucky has already done his changing routine and is a wolf by the time the chief gets there?'' Verna asked.

"Then he can wait and watch Bucky turn back into human shape. Either way, he'll have to believe us. Seeing is believing.''

"Yeah,'' I thought to myself. "If he doesn't lock us all up first.''

Chips solemnly shook hands all around and disappeared back into the woods to take up his position.

We continued up the Pike until we came to the spot where the old road came out of Lost Woods and joined the highway. We were about to turn in when a sudden roaring sound made Huntley and Verna jump. Usually *I'm* the first to jump, but I had heard that sound before. And in the same place, too.

I followed my fellow monster hunters as they dove for cover behind a large tree.

"What is it?'' Verna asked breathlessly.

"A truck,'' I answered.

Sure enough, the same truck I had seen on my way home from Bucky's house roared out onto the highway. And, just as before, the driver didn't switch on the lights until it was rolling along the Pike.

"How did you know it was a truck?" Verna asked me.

I explained.

"Curious," Huntley mumbled softly. "Most curious."

We followed the old road into the woods. When we reached the clearing, Huntley stopped and turned on his flashlight. In its beam, we saw big tire marks in the snow.

"This is where the truck was parked," Huntley pointed out.

"What was it doing in here?" Verna asked. "Hunters?"

"Or maybe trappers?" I suggested. "The ones who set the awful traps Chips is always springing."

Another shriller roaring sound interrupted us. This time no one jumped. That's because the roar was in the distance and moving farther away *into* the woods.

"Another truck?" I wondered out loud.

"Why is it going deeper into the woods?" Verna asked.

"It didn't sound like a truck," Huntley answered, as we began walking toward the old iron bridge.

"There are strange things going on in Lost Woods tonight," he continued in a spooky voice. "And now it's time for us to find out what."

24

The old bridge creaked mournfully as we crossed it. I looked over the side of the rail at the creek below. I couldn't see or hear any water flowing. It was frozen! I wasn't too surprised. The weather *had* been bitterly cold, just as the weatherman had predicted. Now there was nothing to keep the werewolf within the boundaries of Lost Woods.

Nothing but a trio of monster hunters, that is.

On the other side of the bridge, we continued to hike on the old road. When gusts of wind blew snow from the trees in our faces, it felt like slivers of ice. I was glad when the road turned and began its long climb up the hill. We made it to the top and stopped.

"Well, here we are on Werewolf Hill!" Huntley said with relish. "Now, let's go on down the road and look for the mine shaft and the shack."

As we started down the side of the hill, we slipped

and skidded on the icy snow. All I could see in the valley below was dark, thick forest. I raised my eyes to Lookout Hill.

"Please be there watching, Chips," I prayed to myself. "Please!"

The night seemed to get darker as we made our way along. Halfway down, Huntley stopped and pointed silently. We looked and saw that he and the library map had been right. A mine shaft was dug into the side of the hill. Below it, we could see the outline of a small building. Both the shaft and the shack were nestled among the trees and thick clumps of bushes. It was no wonder we hadn't seen them before.

We walked to where the road ended at the shack and made our way through the thick prickly bushes that surrounded it. The bare branches seemed to be

grabbing my coat, telling me to run away while there was still time. I didn't.

The shack was made of wood and looked ancient. The door, though, was still on its hinges. Huntley used his flashlight to check it out.

"Let's hope it's not locked," he whispered.

With that he gingerly climbed the two steps and reached for the knob. The door swung out toward us with an awful creak. We followed Huntley inside.

"Be careful!" he warned. "The floor boards are rotten."

"This whole place is rotten!" Verna muttered.

The shack was small and square and empty. Long since abandoned, like the mine it once served. The other three walls each had a small window in the middle. The glass was gone, of course, so it was just as cold inside as out.

"Good," Huntley exclaimed. "The windows are too small for Bucky to climb out."

"So what do you want me to do?" Verna asked him.

"What do you mean?"

"You said that one of us is going to do something brave. You must mean me. Raymond gets scared watching cartoons on TV."

"But I did mean Raymond," Huntley answered.

"Me?" I gulped.

"We need to get Bucky inside this shack. When he shows up tonight, Raymond will get him to chase him."

"Why me?" I cried.

"Because you're the fastest runner."

That shut me up. He was right.

"Raymond, you'll lead Bucky down here and inside the shack. Then you'll climb out that back window. It's big enough for you to squeeze through but too small for Bucky. Verna and I will slam the door behind him and hold it shut."

"Sounds good to me," Verna agreed.

That was easy for her to say!

"Are you ready?" Huntley asked, putting his gloved hand on my shoulder.

My heart said no but my mouth said yes.

"Good. I know we can count on you. Now go up the hill and wait for Bucky. We'll take our positions here."

We stepped out of the shack and I headed back up the road.

"What do we do if Raymond keeps right on going and doesn't come back?" I heard Verna ask Huntley.

I spun angrily around.

"Don't worry!" I growled. "I'll be back! And I'll tell you something else, Verna Wilkes! I haven't been scared watching cartoons since I left the fifth grade!"

25

The entrance to the mine shaft looked like a dark mouth as I hurried by it. I tried to make myself believe that Chips was at his post over on Lookout Hill, watching me by moonlight. I was still scared but I didn't feel as alone.

At the top of the hill, I slipped behind a large boulder and waited. I was sweating so much I actually felt hot as I crouched in the snow. I didn't have to wait long.

Pretty soon Bucky Bovine came walking down the old road. I waited until he was at my hiding place and then I made my move. I stepped out from behind the boulder and faced him.

"You know something, Bucky?" I said as bravely as I could, since my voice sounded like Mickey Mouse. "If brains were dynamite, you wouldn't have enough to blow your nose."

"Wait until I get my hands on you, Cashew!" Bucky roared.

With that he lunged forward, but I jumped back and began running down the hill. I was so fast and he was so slow that I had to keep running slower so he could keep up.

Ahead I could see the shack. Huntley and Verna were behind the door of our trap, holding it wide open, ready for our prey. Behind me Bucky was yelling and promising to do all kinds of terrible things to me when he caught me.

At the end of the road, I tore through the grabbing bushes. Then I made my mistake. As I jumped toward the open door, I took the old steps too hard. My foot caved in through the second step and I went flying headfirst into the shack. It felt as if my ankle were broken as I struggled to my feet and hobbled to the back window.

Bucky was slow but not *that* slow. I had pulled myself halfway through the open frame when I felt his hand on my rear end pulling me back in. I don't know whether the bang I heard was me hitting the floor or Huntley and Verna slamming the door shut behind Bucky. By then I was in a daze.

"Oh, no! Oh, no!" I heard a scream. "I'm turning into a werewolf!"

Next I heard a snarling sound. Trapped in a shack

in the middle of nowhere with a werewolf! What a terrible end for Raymond Almond, the Always Nervous! I rolled over and looked up, expecting to see Bucky sprouting fur.

What I saw was Bucky the human being standing there staring back at the door. The snarling was coming from *outside* the shack.

Suddenly the door flew open and Huntley and Verna came running *inside*. Huntley pulled the door shut behind them and stood holding onto the doorknob for dear life. Outside, the snarling was growing louder and louder.

Verna stood there looking down at me. "What are you doing in here, Raymond?" she demanded. "You were supposed to crawl out through the window."

"It's a short story," I answered weakly. "I'll tell you about it later if we're alive."

"Well, it's a good thing you *are* in here," she said, "because the werewolf is outside!"

Then she noticed Bucky standing there and her mouth fell open.

"You can't be in here!" she said to him. "You're out there!"

Just then something big and strong and angry hit the side of the shack and filled our ears with the sound of splintering wood.

26

Another awful crash shook the shack. And then another and another and another. Between crashes, the sound of snarling and teeth gnashing added to the terror. The creature outside sounded insane with fury. Another attack split two of the rotten old boards. The whole wall seemed on the verge of crashing in on us.

"Verna!" Huntley called from the door, which he was still holding shut as if his life depended on it. Actually it did, and so did ours!

"What?"

"Come get my flashlight and turn it on so I can see what's happening."

"I'll tell you what's happening," Verna yelled as she snapped on the light. "We're about to be torn to pieces!"

Huntley looked over his shoulder at Bucky.

"It seems I made a slight mistake," he called out above the commotion. "You're obviously not the werewolf."

"There is no werewolf," Bucky shouted back.

"Then what's out *there* trying to get in *here?*" Verna demanded to know. "A cocker spaniel?"

Bucky shook his head.

"It's part wolf, part Siberian husky, part Alaskan malamute," he said.

"I don't care what it is!" I screamed as more wall boards split in toward us. "It sounds mean!"

"It's not just mean," Bucky answered. "It's *real* mean. It was trained that way."

"How do you know so much about it?" Verna asked.

"I've been trying to make friends with it," Bucky replied.

"Bucky?" Huntley called from the door. "*Have* you made friends with it?"

Bucky shrugged his broad shoulders.

"Enough to buy you time to get away. Maybe."

"Maybe is better than nothing," Huntley answered. "What do you suggest?"

"I'll go out there and try to lead it away from here," Bucky said. "Give me a few minutes. If it sounds like the coast is clear, make a run for it."

Bucky moved to the door. Huntley let go of the knob with his right hand and offered it to him. They shook hands. Then, "Ready?" Huntley asked.

"Ready!"

Huntley opened the door and Bucky ran out into the middle of the vicious sounds. Huntley quickly pulled the door shut behind him.

"King! King!" we heard Bucky yelling outside. "Come on, boy! That's a good boy!"

We listened as Bucky led the huge dog away by running through the bushes. The snapping, snarling sounds grew fainter and fainter down the valley.

"All right!" Huntley cried, throwing open the door. "Let's go!"

I tested my ankle and it felt okay. The three of us ran from the shack and headed up the hill.

We had just reached the old road when a shrill, roaring sound stopped us in our tracks. It happened so quickly we only had time to drop to our stomachs in the snow. The sound was coming from the dark entrance to the mine shaft on our left. We watched in amazement as a snowmobile exploded out of the shaft and sped away up the road.

We lay low until the whining sound faded in the distance. This was the same sound we had heard earlier when we first entered the woods.

"Verna?" Huntley said, getting onto his feet and shaking the snow from his thick coat. "Do you still have the flashlight?"

"Don't tell me we're going into that mine?" I gasped as Verna handed Huntley the light.

Huntley didn't answer. He didn't have to. I knew the answer before I even asked the question.

Huntley went first. Verna followed. As usual, Raymond Almond, the Extremely Nervous, brought up the rear.

27

The entrance to the mine shaft was so low we had to stoop down so we wouldn't bang our heads. It was plenty dark, and creepy, too. Outside, the full moon had lighted our path with a pale silvery glow. Inside, the darkness from deep in the mine seemed to be waiting to swallow us up. The thin light from Huntley's flashlight was downright pitiful.

Just inside the entrance, I tripped and fell against Verna. Huntley aimed the flashlight at my feet and we could see metal tracks running straight down the shaft. At the edge of the light, an old coal cart sat waiting to go down.

"Look at those tracks!" Huntley said excitedly. "They're shiny!"

"When they should be rusty," Verna added. "Someone's been running that coal cart over them."

"But why?" I asked. "There's no coal here any

more. It was all mined out years ago.''

We began to walk single file along the tracks, deeper and deeper into the mine. I had been around mines all my life but I had never actually been in one. I was surprised to find the air getting warmer. And then we heard a humming sound. It was faint at first but grew louder as we moved deeper. And then we heard the voices!

Huntley quickly switched off the flashlight and we stopped walking so we could hear better. Several people were talking somewhere farther down the shaft, but we couldn't hear what they were saying.

"Werewolf! Werewolf!'' a voice suddenly screamed.

I sure understood that! I felt my feet moving fast and I figured I must be approaching the mine entrance. That's when I realized I hadn't moved an inch. This was because Verna and Huntley were holding me in place.

"A werewolf in Weehawken?'' another voice from below screamed. "It can't be!''

"What's a Weehawken?'' Verna asked.

"It's a city in New Jersey,'' I explained as they let me go.

"Come on,'' Huntley urged us. "I think I know what's going on down there!''

I have to admit that Verna sort of had to pull me

along as we moved ever deeper into the blackness. The voices kept getting louder and so did the humming sound. The air kept getting warmer, too, and a faint bluish glow began to light up the way ahead. We kept close to the wall as we crept closer to the eerie, flickering light.

Finally we stopped at the entrance to a large carved-out area of the mine. It looked like a big room. I sure didn't expect to see what I saw that night down in that mine shaft.

Television sets! And video-cassette recorders!

They were sitting on old wooden tables. Other tables held more fancy video equipment. By the glow of the TV screens, I could see cables running across the floor to a small generator that hummed in the corner.

Several electric heaters kept the underground room toasty warm.

"What the heck is going on here?" Verna whispered.

"Piracy," Huntley answered. "Video-cassette piracy."

I hung back as Huntley and Verna walked cautiously into the room.

"I'll stay here and keep watch," I called softly.

Sentry duty seemed the best job for Raymond, the by now Practically Hysterical. It was a good thing, too! As Huntley and Verna reached the center of the room, a huge man wearing a checked flannel shirt jumped out of the shadows and grabbed them around their necks with his powerful-looking arms.

"Let go!" Verna cried as she began to struggle. "I know karate!"

"I'm J. Huntley English, M.H." Huntley's voice was firm. "And I demand you release us immediately!"

"*You* shut up!" the man roared. "And *you* stop wiggling or I'll break you both in half!" He looked as if he could do it, too. I was glad to see Huntley and Verna doing as they were told.

"Did anyone else come down here with you?" the man asked angrily, as he looked back at the entrance where I was hiding against the wall.

I didn't wait to hear their answer. I turned and slipped away back up the mine shaft as if an army of Bucky Bovines were on my tail.

Halfway to the entrance, I saw the beam of a flash-light coming down at me. I prayed it was Police Chief Murphy, but I dove into a tiny side passage until I could make sure. As the figure walked by my hiding place and on down the shaft, I gasped in surprise. It was Barney Beeker, the owner of Barney Beeker's Bargain Emporium! I knew that the only business he could have in a mine in the middle of Lost Woods at night was bad business. I waited until he had disap-peared down the shaft before finishing my dash up to the entrance.

Air had never smelled better than the air I sucked in that night after I ran out of the mine. I stood staring over at the dark outline of Lookout Hill. Somehow I had to signal Chips Chipaletta that it was time to go for help. But how? I had no flashlight or matches. I began jumping up and down, waving my arms and hoping he would recognize me by the light of the moon.

That's when I noticed the outline of a tall man walking toward me down the road. Since Police Chief Murphy is tall, I knew that's who it had to be.

When the figure reached me, I recognized him. But it wasn't the chief! It was that customer from the video store again. I turned and bolted.

"Hey, kid!" the man called. "Wait a minute!"

In a panic I ran back inside the mine shaft. Once inside, I realized my mistake. Now I was trapped! My only hope was to hide near the entrance and make the man think I had run back down the shaft. And the only place I could see to hide was the coal cart that was sitting on the tracks.

I ran straight for it and vaulted over the top, landing with a thud inside. I then realized with horror that I was moving! The impact of my jump had started the cart down the track into the mine.

"Hey, kid!" I heard the man yell. "Stop!"

"I wish I could!" I yelled back.

In just a second the cart was roaring down the tracks so fast I didn't dare jump. If the runaway coal cart had a brake, I couldn't find it. Finally I gave up feeling for it and dared look over the top in the direction I was going.

Several years ago my parents took me to Disneyland.

There's a ride there called Space Mountain. It's this roller coaster you ride in the dark. It was the scariest ride I had ever been on. Until that night I went speeding out of control down the mine shaft.

Ahead I could see a pinprick of light. As the cart rolled on faster and faster, the light got bigger and bigger. I realized that it was a flashlight.

"Runaway cart!" I yelled. "Get out of the way!"

The flashlight holder dove to the side as the cart roared past him. As I flew by, I saw by the light

that it was Mr. Beeker rolling against the wall.

Now another light appeared in the distance. It was the flickering bluish glow of the television monitors in the underground room. I knew that my terrifying trip was about to come to a terrifying end.

In another second the cart left the rails and went flying through the chamber. The only person I saw was the burly man. He was standing in the path of the runaway cart as if he couldn't believe his eyes. He didn't stand there for long. If he had, he wouldn't have lived to be sent to prison. With a scream, he dove straight into one of the tables filled with equipment.

I don't remember much about the crash that followed. First the cart destroyed a bin full of video cassettes. Then it plowed through a pile of electronic equipment in a shower of sparks and explosions. And then it hit the wall. To say that I came to a sudden halt would be a terrible understatement!

Lucky for me that coal cart had been built to last. It was plenty sturdy and it held together as it bounced off the wall and stopped.

As I lay in a daze on the bottom of the cart, I could hear this voice.

"Oh, no! Oh, no!" the voice was screaming. "I'm turning into a werewolf!"

"Who cares?" I remember saying to myself.

29

The next thing I knew, Huntley and Verna were helping me out of the cart.

"That was the bravest thing I've ever seen!" Verna exclaimed as she patted me on the back. "Riding that coal cart down here to save us!"

"It was nothing," I said modestly.

Actually, I was swallowing hard to keep from throwing up. I looked over to where the big man was lying across the table. A television monitor had fallen on his back and he was out cold.

"Thank goodness you're all right!" a voice cried from the entrance to the room.

I looked over and saw the stranger who had chased me come walking in. In the light, he looked young and clean cut in his dark blue parka. He was pulling Mr. Beeker along with him. As they got closer, I could see that Mr. Beeker was handcuffed.

When the stranger saw the big man draped over

the table, he quickly handcuffed him, too, and then lifted the television off him.

"Excuse me, sir," Huntley said, offering his hand. "I'm J. Huntley English, M.H."

"I'm Gary Teeter, FBI," the man said as they shook hands.

"I take it you've been investigating this video-cassette piracy ring?" Huntley asked.

"Correct. I knew Beeker here was selling illegal video cassettes out of his store. I *didn't* know he was actually involved with producing the cassettes. I decided to follow him tonight and he led me here."

"What's video-cassette piracy, anyway?" Verna asked.

"It's making illegal copies of movies on video cassettes and then selling them," Agent Teeter answered.

"But why would anyone want to buy illegal video cassette movies when they can buy legal ones at a video store?" I asked.

"Because the video-cassette pirates can sell their movies much cheaper," Huntley explained. "You see, the pirates duplicate movies secretly and illegally, so they don't have to pay any of the people who were responsible for making the movie."

"And they don't have to pay any of the companies that *legally* own the rights to produce video cassettes," Agent Teeter added.

"So all this equipment was being used to duplicate

video-cassette movies illegally?'' Verna asked.

"That's right," Huntley answered. "I figure they did the copying down here and then sent the finished video cassettes up the mine shaft in the coal cart. Then they used snowmobiles to carry the cassettes out of the woods to the highway.''

"That truck out there!" I said snapping my fingers. "It was picking up the video cassettes and hauling them away.''

Agent Teeter nodded his head.

"They were shipping and selling their illegal movies all over the eastern part of the country. Beeker here made his big mistake when he got greedy and began selling his illegal video cassettes out of his own store. That's what brought me to Barkley and then to this mine.''

Beeker shook his head grimly and stared at his feet.

I walked over to the smashed bin and sifted through the cassettes that were scattered all over the floor.

"These are all 'I Wed a Werewolf from Weehawken,' " I pointed out.

"I'm not surprised," the FBI agent declared. "It's a hot movie in the video business today.''

At that moment Chips Chipaletta walked in with Police Chief Murphy.

"I didn't see your signal but I got worried and brought the chief here anyway," Chips explained.

"What's going on?" Chief Murphy demanded.

Agent Teeter introduced himself and explained. Meanwhile, the big man on the table had regained consciousness and stood up unsteadily on his feet.

"I can't say I'm surprised to hear that Bull Bovine here is involved in this," Chief Murphy said. "But I am surprised at you, Barney."

"Bull Bovine?" I asked. "Is he any relation to Bucky Bovine?"

"Bull is Bucky's father."

"Oh, my gosh!" Huntley cried. "We forgot about Bucky! Come on, gang!"

30

The gang turned out to be Huntley, Verna, Chips, and me. Agent Teeter and Chief Murphy had to wrap things up at the mine and take the prisoners to jail.

The four of us ran down to the shack, where we picked up Bucky's trail. Using his flashlight, Huntley found Bucky's footprints in the snow. They disappeared down the hill. They were followed by huge paw prints. I shuddered.

"That beast may have torn him apart by now," Verna said.

Leave it to Verna always to look at the dark side of things.

We followed the trail down into the valley and then struggled up to the top of Lookout Hill. We knew the way from there down to the bottom. Mournful whining cries were coming from beyond the trees. We hurried through them to the path by the creek.

That's where we found Bucky. He was sitting beside the huge dog, cradling its giant head in his lap. Huntley ran up and shone his flashlight down and we could see why the dog was moaning. Its front leg was bent and bloody.

"What happened?" Huntley asked, as he knelt beside Bucky.

"It stepped in a trap," Bucky answered angrily.

And then he noticed Chips standing nearby.

"One of *your* traps, Chipaletta, you creep!" he yelled.

"My traps?" Chips cried in anger. "I don't set traps. I come out here and spring them. *You're* the one who sets them!"

"Me?" Bucky said in surprise. "I don't set them. I come out here and spring them, too."

Huntley raised his hand.

"I think you two have been on the same side all along and didn't know it. Now you're going to have to work *together* to save this dog.

"We need to get him to a veterinarian," Bucky said, "but he's too heavy for me to carry alone."

"Let me help!" Chips said, kneeling down.

The dog gave a long, low growl.

"Careful!" I warned. "He'll bite your hand off!"

"No, he won't," Chips answered with confidence. "He knows we're trying to help him."

The huge dog growled and snapped its jaws as Bucky and Chips gently began to lift him but made no move to bite them. When they staggered under the weight, Verna moved in to help. And then even I joined in. Huntley led the way, lighting the path with his flashlight. Together, we carried the dreaded werewolf out of Lost Woods.

31

We carried the dog back to the Chipaletta trailer. As we laid him down on the kitchen floor, Mrs. Chipaletta wrapped him in a blanket and Chips got on the phone and called Dr. Nezvesky at his home. The veterinarian drove right out and then sent all of us kids away from the kitchen. We gathered in Chips's bedroom and, while we waited, tried to piece the rest of the mystery together.

"Bucky?" Huntley said, putting his hand gently on the big boy's shoulder. "I'm sorry to have to tell you that your father's been arrested for video-cassette piracy."

"Really?" Bucky sighed deeply. "Boy, am I glad!"

"You are?" I cried.

"Maybe we should start at the beginning," Huntley suggested. "Raymond? Remember when you came to tell me Chips's story about a werewolf in Lost Woods?"

"Yeah. And you told me you already knew about it."

"I did. Bucky had been to see me with a similar story. As he was my client, I couldn't reveal this to you."

"I had been out in the woods springing traps, trying to save animals," Bucky explained. "I saw this man in the distance, and then he disappeared and what looked like a wolf was there instead. I don't believe in things like werewolves, but I had seen it with my own eyes."

"So Bucky came to me and asked me to find out if what he saw was a werewolf or a real wolf."

"I had to know for sure which it really was." Bucky picked up the story. "If it was a werewolf, I was going to let the Monster Hunter here take care of it. But if it was a real wolf, *I* was going to try and help it."

"Help it?" I asked.

"I've read a lot about wolves," Bucky explained. "They're wonderful animals. But they've had a lot of bad publicity. I knew that if word got out that a wolf was living in Lost Woods, everyone would be scared. And pretty soon hunters would show up with guns.

"Where does your dad come into all this?" Verna asked.

122

"I continued my own investigation," Bucky went on. "One night I heard voices and screams. They seemed to be coming from the area where I had seen the man disappear and the wolf appear. So I went to that hill to look around. I found the mine shaft and went in. That's when I ran into my father. Boy, was I surprised!"

"Really?" Chips wondered.

"I hadn't seen him in years. He and Mom were divorced when I was little. He'd been real mean to us and we were glad when he moved out. That night, he took me down in the mine and showed me what he was doing. Then he warned me that if I said anything to anybody he would hurt Mom. Just to make sure I wouldn't talk, he made me help him duplicate videos. Then he told me that made me just as guilty as he was."

"Nice guy," Verna muttered.

"So that's why you stormed into Huntley's office and told him to stay out of Lost Woods?" I asked.

Bucky nodded.

"I was afraid if you guys kept snooping around out here you'd find out the truth and Dad would blame me."

"Now that I *know* the truth, I can't believe I thought there was a werewolf wandering around," Chips commented. "I feel stupid!"

"Don't feel that way, Chips," Huntley consoled him. "I actually came to believe that Bucky *was* the werewolf. And don't forget that King *is* part wolf."

"Dad picked him up somewhere and taught him to be mean," Bucky added. "When Dad or Mr. Beeker went away from the mine, they kept him tied up near the entrance as a watchdog. When they were in the mine they let him loose to wander around and keep people like Chips and me away. They trained him not to cross the creeks and leave the woods."

"Don't forget," Huntley pointed out. "When all of us saw what we thought was a werewolf transformation, we were standing a long way off and it was dark. We couldn't see what was really happening. All we saw was a man standing there. Then he was gone and a wolf was there. We didn't know that it was Bull Bovine stooping down near the trees to unleash his watchdog before he snuck over to the mine entrance. And then there were those weird voices screaming about werewolves."

"Mr. Beeker and Mr. Bovine were down in the mine testing the video cassettes they had copied," I said. "Right?"

"Right," Huntley answered. "They must have figured that night was the safest time to try some of them out. I guess they didn't realize how much the mine shaft amplified and carried the sound."

"How's King?" Bucky cried as Dr. Nezvesky stepped into the room.

"He's going to be fine," the veterinarian replied. "But he's going to need a lot of care. A lot of love wouldn't hurt, either. It looks as if he's been abused most of his life."

"You know something, Doctor?" Huntley said with a smile. "I think there are two people in this room who can handle that."

32

And so we wrapped up what I now call "The Case of the Wandering Werewolf." Bull Bovine and Barney Beeker were sentenced to prison terms. Agent Teeter and Chief Murphy waited out on the old road in Lost Woods for the truck driver to return. The driver must have heard about the raid, because he or she never came back.

Bucky and Chips have become best friends and spend their time nursing injured animals back to health and educating people on the cruelties of animal trapping. King lives out at Bucky's, where he's doing fine. Bucky keeps him close to the house because the big dog still doesn't trust most people. The last time I was out there, though, he actually licked my hand. The dog did. Not Bucky.

Several days after the bust, I stopped by to see Huntley. I found him in his office being interviewed by Marilyn Possner, a reporter for the *Observer-*

Reporter. Huntley had his cassette player and VCR set up next to each other.

"Hello, Raymond," Mrs. Possner greeted me. "Huntley was just telling me how all of you worked together to break up that video-cassette-pirating operation."

I smiled. Good old Huntley! He always makes sure everyone gets credit.

"Huntley? I'm ready for your demonstration," she then said.

Huntley went over and fast-forwarded a video cassette that was in the VCR. When he stopped it and pressed the play button, we looked at the TV screen.

A man was standing on a street looking up at a full moon. Gradually he began sprouting hair and big teeth.

"Oh, no! Oh, no!" he screamed. "I'm turning into a werewolf!"

Which he did. I had to admit that the special effects were great.

A few minutes later, two women came walking down the street toward the man.

"Werewolf! Werewolf!" one of the women yelled, pointing at the hairy fellow.

"A werewolf in Weehawken?" the other woman screamed. "It can't be!"

Huntley then stopped the VCR and pushed the play button on his cassette player. It was the tape he had made the night he and I had seen Bucky Bovine in Lost Woods.

"Oh, no! Oh, no!" the same man was yelling again. "I'm turning into a werewolf!"

Huntley quickly turned off the cassette player before Mrs. Possner could hear my bad case of nerves that followed on the tape.

"I can't believe I thought that was Bucky Bovine's voice," I said, shaking my head.

"The power of suggestion can do funny things, Raymond," Mrs. Possner noted.

"I know," I admitted. "But if I hadn't panicked and run that night in the woods, we would have been there to hear that woman yelling about a werewolf in Weehawken. At that point, Huntley would have known we were hearing a video cassette."

"Maybe so, Raymond," Huntley said with a smile, "but just think of all the excitement we would have missed."

I shook my head.

"After what we've been through, the only excitement I want for the rest of the winter is to sit around and watch the snow melt."

Mrs. Possner laughed.

"Can I quote you on that, Raymond?"

"Definitely," I answered with a wink.